THE LION
AND THE MOUSE

by
Aesop

Illustrated by
Bob Dole

Troll Associates

Library of Congress Cataloging in Publication Data

Aesopus.
    The lion and the mouse.

      SUMMARY: A little mouse saves the life of the
King of the Beasts.
      [1. Fables]   I. Dole, Bob. II. Title.
PZ8.2.A255Li 1981   398.2'452   80-28154
ISBN 0-89375-466-8
ISBN 0-89375-467-6 (pbk.)

THE LION
AND THE MOUSE

One day, a long time ago, a lion decided to take a short nap. It was too hot outside, so he went into his den, where it was cool and comfortable. He stretched out and rested his head on his front legs. Soon he was fast asleep.

Before long, a little mouse peeked out from the corner of the lion's den. When the lion did not move, the mouse grew bolder. Soon he was scurrying about. Closer and closer he came to the huge lion. Suddenly, for no reason at all, he ran right over the lion's paw and up onto his nose!

The King of Beasts awoke at once, but he did not move a muscle. Slowly, he opened one eye. Then he

quickly brought his huge paw down and captured the
tiny creature.

The mouse was terrified. He squeaked and squealed. Then he begged for mercy. "Please, King of Beasts," he cried, "do not take my life. Spare me, and I will never forget your act of kindness."

"Spare you?" roared the lion. "First you dare to awaken me, and then you ask me for a favor! Give me one good reason why I should not eat you this very instant!"

"The day may come," replied the mouse, "when I can do a favor for *you*. You never know when you will need the help of someone like me."

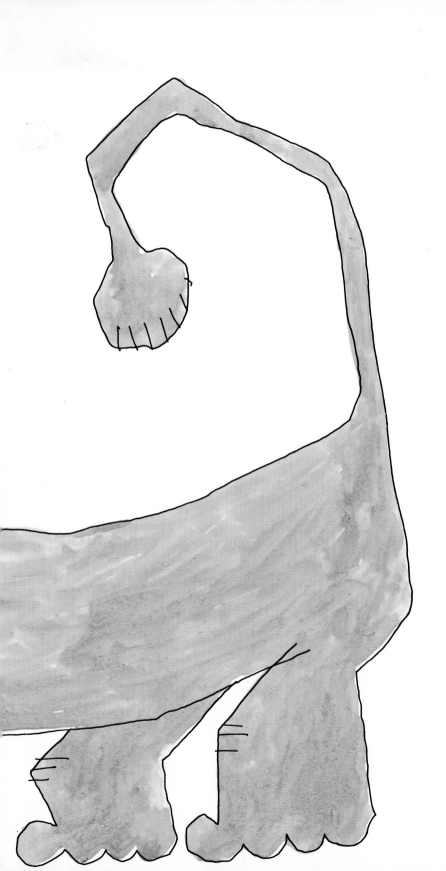

The lion began to smile. He could not help himself. The very idea! How could a tiny mouse ever help the King of Beasts?

The lion was so amused that he let the little mouse go.

The mouse scampered away and disappeared into a dark corner. The lion closed his eyes and went back to sleep.

And he forgot all about the little mouse.

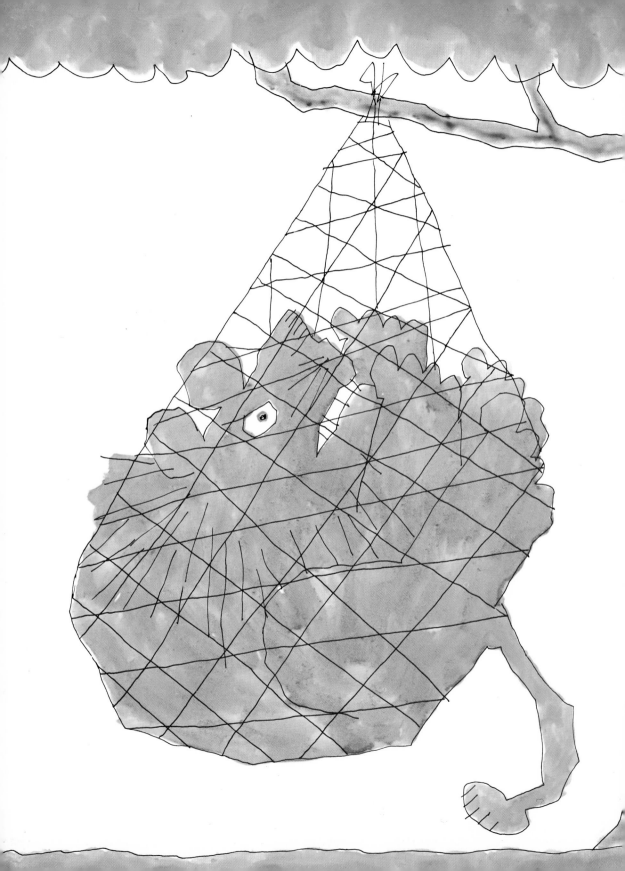

One day, the lion was out hunting for food. He did not know that some hunters had set out a net to try to catch him. Suddenly, the King of Beasts was caught in the net!

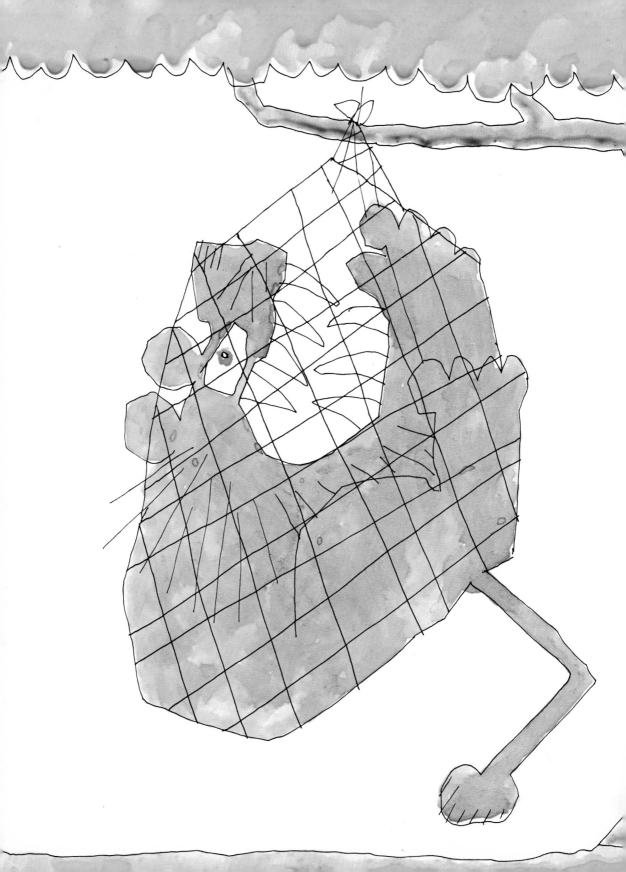

He fought to get free. But no matter how he struggled, he became more and more tangled in the net. He growled, and he snarled. Then he let out a roar that was so terrible it echoed far and near.

In a distant part of the forest, the tiny mouse stopped what he was doing and listened. He heard the lion's roar, and he recognized the voice of the lion who had once spared his life.

So he scampered off through the forest.

He found the King of Beasts struggling helplessly in the tangled net.

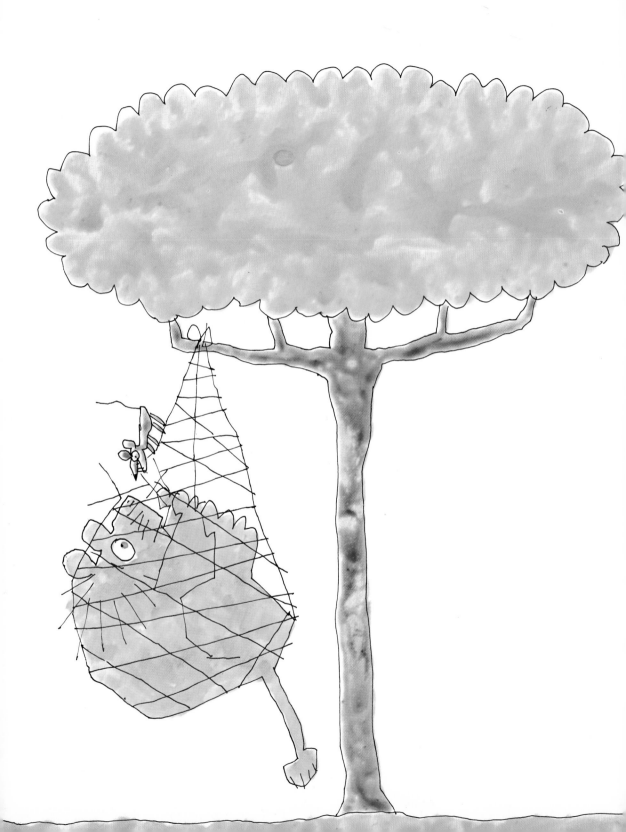

"Greetings, Your Majesty," said the mouse. "You seem to be tied up at the moment. But perhaps I can help set you free." And without another word, he set to work nibbling and gnawing at the ropes of the net.

Before long, the net began to weaken, and there was a
hole large enough for the lion to wriggle out.

Then the lion remembered what the little mouse had once said to him. *"You never know when you will need the help of someone like me."* And the lion smiled, for those very words had come true—the tiny mouse had saved the life of the King of Beasts!